ANIMAL **ANTICS** A **TO** Z.

Eddie Elephant's Exciting Egg-Sitting

by Barbara deRubertis • illustrated by R.W. Alley

THE KANE PRESS / NEW YORK

Alpha Betty's Class

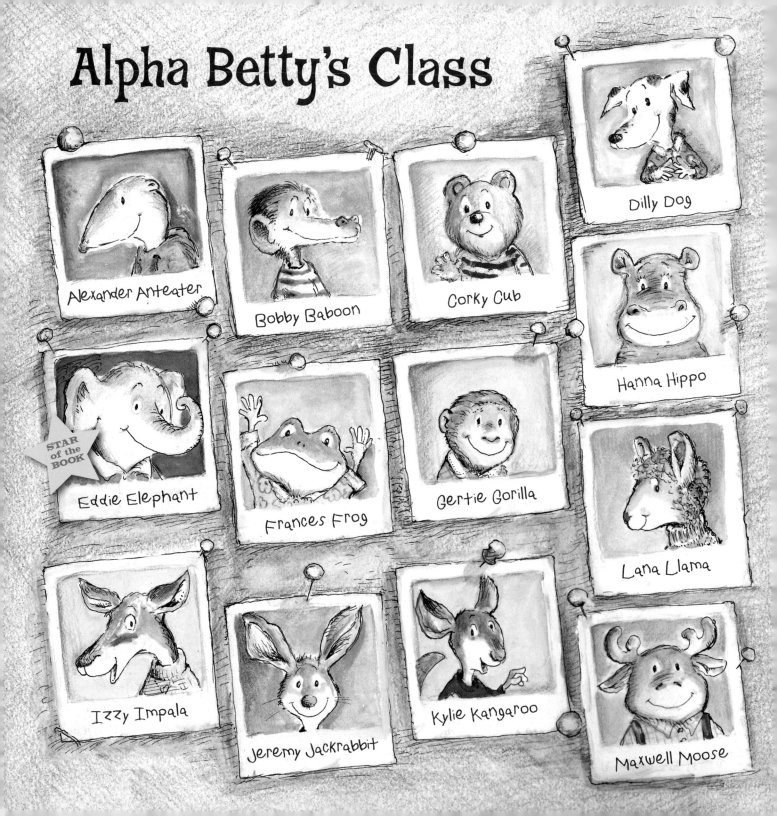

Library of Congress Cataloging-in-Publication Data

deRubertis, Barbara.
Eddie Elephant's exciting egg-sitting / by Barbara deRubertis ; illustrated by R.W. Alley.
p. cm. — (Animal antics A to Z)
Summary: Eddie Elephant loves to tell stories, which keeps him from getting bored when he is
asked to help egg-sit for his neighbors, Elmer and Ernestine Emu.
ISBN 978-1-57565-316-7 (library binding : alk. paper) — ISBN 978-1-57565-309-9 (pbk. : alk. paper)
[1. Storytelling—Fiction. 2. Eggs—Fiction. 3. Elephants—Fiction. 4. Emus—Fiction. 5. Alphabet.
6. Humorous stories.] I. Alley, R. W. (Robert W.), ill. II. Title.
PZ7.D4475Edd 2010
[E]—dc22   2009049878

1 3 5 7 9 10 8 6 4 2

First published in the United States of America in 2010 by Kane Press, Inc.
Printed in the United States of America
WOZ0710

Series Editor: Juliana Hanford
Book Design: Edward Miller

Animal Antics A to Z is a registered trademark of Kane Press, Inc.

www.kanepress.com

Eddie Elephant loved attending
Alpha Betty's school.

Math was not easy for Eddie.
Reading was not easy, either.

But Eddie was VERY good
at telling stories.

He could tell stories about
elephant emperors.

And elephant explorers.

He could tell stories about
fearless elephants.

And enchanted elephants.

Everybody in Eddie's class enjoyed
his stories.

Alpha Betty said that Eddie was a
"born storyteller."

Eddie was also a helpful elephant.

After school, he enjoyed helping his neighbors, Elmer and Ernestine Emu.

Ernestine was an excellent cook.
She even starred in her own TV
cooking show!

Elmer Emu was an expert gardener.
He grew veggies for Ernestine's recipes.

Eddie Elephant helped Elmer plant seeds.
He helped Elmer pull weeds.

And Elmer sent Eddie home
with free veggies every day.

One day Elmer seemed very excited
when Eddie arrived.

"Eddie! Look!" Elmer exclaimed.
He pointed at the Emus' nest.

"Wow!" said Eddie.
"What an enormous green egg!"

"Yes!" said Elmer.
"Ernestine laid it this morning
before she went to work.

Now it's my job to care for the egg.
That's what emu daddies do!"

"I will need your help, Eddie," said Elmer.
"You can be my egg-sitter after school while
I tend to the garden.

You can help me keep the egg nice and warm.
But please sit on it VERY gently!"

At first, Eddie Elephant did not like the idea
of egg-sitting. It did not seem very exciting!

He preferred planting seeds or pulling weeds.

However, he agreed to help Elmer with the egg.

It was NOT easy being an egg-sitter.
Eddie was small for an elephant.

But he was still an ELEPHANT!

He sat this way.

He sat that way.

He sat every which way.

Nothing seemed exactly right.

Finally Eddie decided to wrap his trunk
around the egg.

Then Eddie relaxed.
He began to entertain the egg by
telling stories.

Eddie told stories about elephant emperors.

And elephant explorers.

20

He told stories about fearless elephants.

And enchanted elephants.

Eventually Eddie became an
expert egg-sitter.

One day, after weeks and weeks of egg-sitting,
Eddie received a big surprise.

As he was telling a story, the egg trembled.
Then it began to crack.

Eddie felt nervous.
He even felt a little scared.

He was about to call for Elmer
when . . .

. . . the egg cracked open! And a baby emu emerged!
Eddie was elated. He gently picked up the baby emu.

The baby emu exclaimed, "Daddy?"

"No," Eddie said.
"I'm your friend, Eddie.
Here comes your daddy!"

Elmer eagerly welcomed his new
baby emu.

"Ernestine will be SO pleased!"
Elmer beamed.

"Thank you, Eddie. You are an
excellent egg-sitter!"

Now Eddie Elephant speeds home to see the Emu family every day after school.

Elmer plants seeds and pulls weeds.

Ernestine experiments with recipes for her TV show.

And Eddie and little Emma Lou Emu entertain them by telling stories.

Emma Lou can tell stories about emu empresses.

And emu explorers.

She can tell stories about
fearless emus.

And enchanted emus.

Emma Lou is very good at telling stories.

Eddie Elephant says Emma Lou is a "born storyteller!"

FUN FACTS

- Home: Tropical areas of Africa and Asia
- Weight: African elephants can weigh up to 16,000 pounds. They are the largest animals living on land. Asian elephants weigh up to 11,000 pounds.
- Favorite foods: Grass, leaves, fruit . . . and up to 50 gallons of water each day! Elephants drink by sucking up water in their trunks and squirting it into their mouths.
- **Did You Know?** When the weather is too hot, elephants flap their huge ears to cool off.

For fun facts about **emus**, visit www.kanepress.com/AnimalAntics/EddieElephant.html

LOOK BACK

- The word *egg* <u>begins</u> with a *short e* sound. Listen to the words on pages 6–7 being read again. When you hear a word that <u>begins</u> with the *short e*, pat your head and say the word.
- The word *green* has a *long e* sound. Listen to the words on page 15 being read again. When you hear a word that has the *long e* sound, pull your ear and say the word.
- **Bonus!** Listen to page 22 being read again. When you hear a word with the *long e* sound, stretch your hands apart. When you hear a word with the *short e* sound, bring your hands together. Which word has TWO *long e* sounds?

TRY THIS!

- Cut out six egg-shaped pieces of paper.* Write one of the consonants *d, h, m, p, t* in **black** on each of five eggs. Then write *en* in green on the sixth egg. Place each of the consonant eggs in front of the *en* egg one at a time . . . and sound out the five words you can make.
- Cut out six more egg-shaped pieces of paper. Write one of the consonants *b, g, l, m, s* in **black** on each of five eggs. Then write *et* in green on the last egg. Again, place each of the consonant eggs in front of the *et* egg one at a time . . . and sound out the five words you can make.

*A printable, ready-to-use activity page with 12 egg shapes is available at: www.kanepress.com/AnimalAntics/EddieElephant.html

FOR MORE ACTIVITIES, go to Eddie Elephant's website: www.kanepress.com/AnimalAntics/EddieElephant.html
You'll also find a recipe for Ernestine Emu's Cheese & Veggie Omelet!